July Jitters

The mayor announced that the pet contest would begin in three minutes. "ALL PETS AND THEIR OWNERS MUST LINE UP NOW!" he yelled through his bullhorn.

Lucy and Brian tied the three-cornered hat to the wig. Bradley set the wig on Polly's head and tied it on. Then he and Lucy taped the tinfoil buckles on to Polly's front hooves.

Nate and Bradley laid the Declaration of Independence on Pal's back like a cape. They tied it to his collar and tail.

"They look awesome!" Bradley said.

"I sure hope the mayor thinks so," Nate said.

"ONE MORE MINUTE!" the mayor cried.

Everyone turned to look at him.

And that was when Polly and Pal took off running.

Calendar Mysteries

July Jitters

WITHDRAWN

by Ron Roy

illustrated by
John Steven Gurney

A STEPPING STONE BOOK™

Random House 🏠 New York

This one is for Christy Webster.
—R.R.

To Riley, thanks for posing!
—J.S.G.

Text copyright © 2012 by Ron Roy
Cover art, map, and interior illustrations copyright © 2012 by John Steven Gurney

Visit us on the Web!
ronroy.com
randomhouse.com/kids

Educators and librarians, for a variety of teaching tools,
visit us at randomhouse.com/teachers

Library of Congress Cataloging-in-Publication Data
Roy, Ron.
July jitters / by Ron Roy ; illustrated by John Steven Gurney.
  p. cm. — (Calendar mysteries)
"A Stepping Stone Book."
Summary: Bradley, Brian, Nate, and Lucy enter Polly the pony and Pal the dog in a July 4th pet costume contest, but when Independence Day arrives the animals are nowhere to be found.
ISBN 978-0-375-86882-5 (trade) — ISBN 978-0-375-96882-2 (lib. bdg.) —
ISBN 978-0-375-89965-2 (ebook)
[1. Mystery and detective stories. 2. Lost and found possessions—Fiction. 3. Fourth of July—Fiction. 4. Ponies—Fiction. 5. Dogs—Fiction. 6. Twins—Fiction. 7. Brothers and sisters—Fiction. 8. Cousins—Fiction.] I. Gurney, John Steven, ill. II. Title.
PZ7.R8139 Jul 2011 [Fic]—dc23 2011025276

Printed in the United States of America

10 9 8

Contents

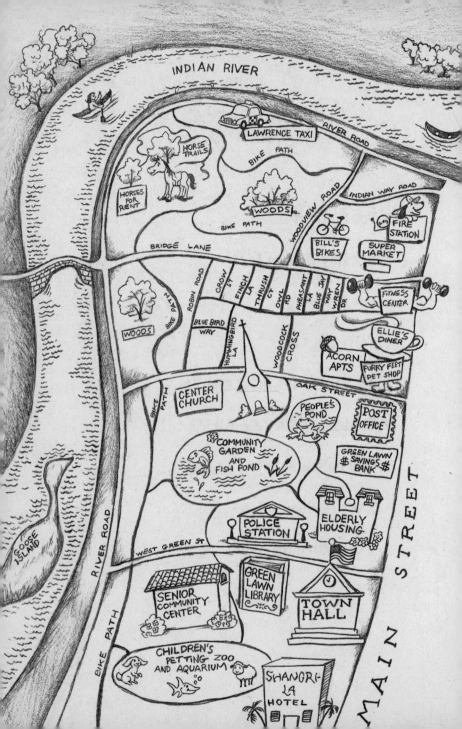

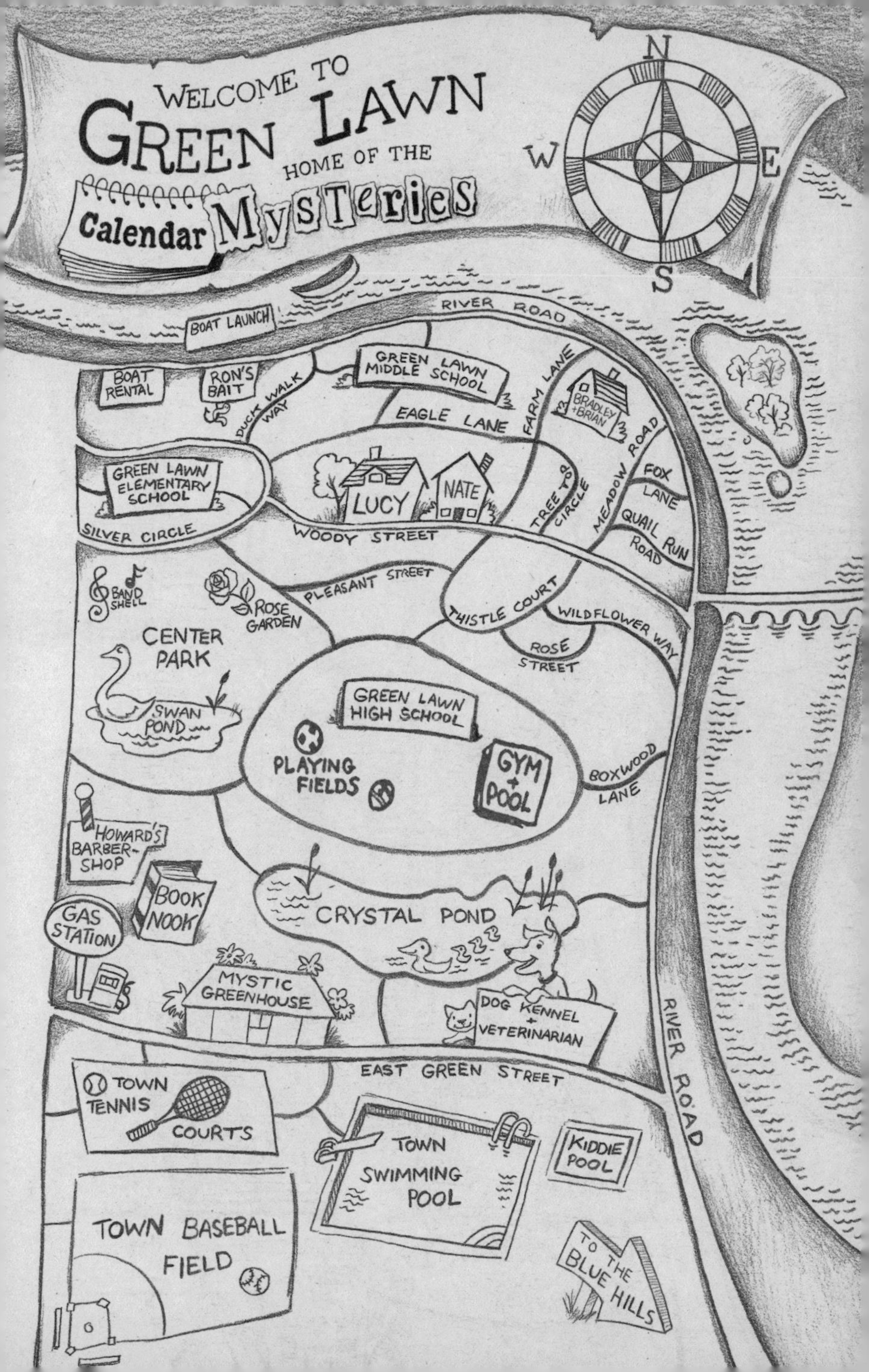
WELCOME TO
GREEN LAWN
HOME OF THE
Calendar Mysteries
N
W
E
S
BOAT LAUNCH
RIVER ROAD
BOAT RENTAL
RON'S BAIT
DUCK WALK WAY
GREEN LAWN MIDDLE SCHOOL
EAGLE LANE
FARM LANE
BRADLEY + BRIAN
MEADOW ROAD
GREEN LAWN ELEMENTARY SCHOOL
LUCY
NATE
TREE TOP CIRCLE
FOX LANE
QUAIL RUN ROAD
SILVER CIRCLE
WOODY STREET
BAND SHELL
ROSE GARDEN
PLEASANT STREET
THISTLE COURT
WILDFLOWER WAY
ROSE STREET
CENTER PARK
SWAN POND
GREEN LAWN HIGH SCHOOL
PLAYING FIELDS
GYM + POOL
BOXWOOD LANE
HOWARD'S BARBER-SHOP
BOOK NOOK
GAS STATION
CRYSTAL POND
MYSTIC GREENHOUSE
DOG KENNEL + VETERINARIAN
RIVER ROAD
EAST GREEN STREET
TOWN TENNIS COURTS
TOWN SWIMMING POOL
KIDDIE POOL
TOWN BASEBALL FIELD
TO THE BLUE HILLS

1
Pet Contest

"Can you guess who I am?" Mr. Vooray asked the students in his first-grade class.

He was wearing a white wig with a ponytail tied with a ribbon. On top of the wig sat a hat with three corners. He wore short pants, showing long white socks. Shiny buckles decorated the tops of his shoes.

"Elvis Presley?" Nate Hathaway asked.

Mr. Vooray shook his head. "I'm a king, but not the king of rock and roll," he said, grinning. "Anyone else have a guess?"

"King Tut?" Brian Pinto said.

Everyone laughed.

"Wrong period of history," Mr. Vooray said. "And King Tut was nine years old when he became king. Do I look that young?"

It was the last day of school, and warm in the classroom. Because of snow days, school was letting out late this year. A fan sat on Mr. Vooray's desk, but it didn't do much good. The windows were open, but there was no breeze.

"Give us a hint!" one boy called out.

"Okay, I will," said Mr. Vooray. He pulled a stack of play money off the math shelf. He handed it to Bradley Pinto, who sat in the first row. "Pass it out, and make sure everyone gets some, Bradley."

Bradley walked down the rows, giving play paper money to all the kids.

"Does everyone have money?" Mr. Vooray asked when Bradley was back in his seat.

"But it's fake!" Brian Pinto said. "We can't buy anything with it."

"Pretend," Mr. Vooray said. Then he pulled a box of prizes off the game shelf. "Lucy, do you want to come up here and buy something with your money?"

Lucy Armstrong walked to the front of the class. She looked in the box. "Can I buy those stickers?" she asked.

"Certainly," Mr. Vooray said. "That will be one dollar, please."

Lucy handed him a fake dollar.

"And ten dollars tax, please," Mr. Vooray added.

"Ten dollars tax!" Lucy said. "That's a lot!"

"Do you want the stickers, Lucy?" Mr. Vooray asked.

"I guess so," Lucy said. She gave him ten more dollars and took the stickers back to her seat.

"You got robbed!" Nate told her.

"Has anyone guessed which king I am?" asked Mr. Vooray.

"King Robber!" Brian said, and everyone laughed again.

"I am King George the Third," Mr. Vooray said.

"Who's he?" Nate asked.

"He ruled Great Britain back in the

1700s," Mr. Vooray explained. "That included the American colonies. A lot of the king's subjects didn't think he was a very good king. For one thing, he taxed them way too much, just like I taxed Lucy too much. Even though the people in the colonies paid high taxes, they didn't have anyone to represent them in the British government. They had made a new life for themselves. They had built homes, worked on farms, and started families. But even from far away, King George still tried to rule them."

"How could he do that?" Lucy asked.

"He was a very powerful king," Mr. Vooray said. "He had lots of money, ships, and men who could cross the ocean and keep an eye on the colonists. Finally, the colonists had had enough of King George. They decided to break away from his power. In 1776, they asked Thomas Jefferson to write a paper explaining why it was a good idea to declare independence from King George. We call this paper the Declaration of Independence."

"Hey, I saw that!" Scott yelled out. "It's in Washington, D.C. Right, Mr. Vooray?"

"Yes, but the original is quite faded and almost impossible to read," the teacher said. "Remember, it was written almost two hundred forty years ago."

"But if it was so long ago, why do we have parades and fireworks on July Fourth?" a girl named Sue asked.

"When the colonists separated from the king to form the United States, they celebrated," Mr. Vooray explained. "And we still celebrate every July Fourth. Everyone wants to remember the importance of Independence Day."

"Are you going to the parade?" Bradley asked.

"I wouldn't miss it," the teacher said.

"I'm going to enter my parrot, Patrick, in the mayor's pet contest."

"What contest?" Brian asked.

"It's the mayor's idea," Mr. Vooray said. "Before the real parade starts, there will be a pet parade. The mayor wants people to bring their pets, dressed as someone from 1776. The winner gets a prize. It costs a dollar to enter a pet, and the money goes to the food pantry."

"What's the prize?" a boy named Seth asked.

"The owner of the winning pet gets to be mayor for a day," Mr. Vooray said. "Pretty cool, right?"

"You mean, like, sit in the mayor's office all day?" Jackie asked.

Mr. Vooray grinned. "You'd also get to drive around in his shiny black car and eat lunch in his favorite restaurant," he said. "Plus, you'd be on TV. The local TV station will be filming the whole thing."

"On TV!" a bunch of kids yelled. They all started chattering about how they would dress their hamsters, cats, and canaries.

"Way cool!" Brian said. "We can enter our dog! If he wins, I get to be mayor!"

"But we both own Pal," Bradley said. "If Pal wins, we both get to be mayor, right, Mr. Vooray?"

Mr. Vooray smiled. "I think my parrot is going to win," he said.

2
Bradley Has an Idea

The next day was July 1. Bradley, Brian, Nate, and Lucy were in the Pintos' barn, where it was cool. They were sitting on bales of hay. Pigeons made cooing noises in the roof rafters over their heads.

The four kids were best buddies. The twins' older brother, Josh, was friends with Nate's sister, Ruth Rose, and Lucy's cousin Dink Duncan. Lucy was visiting from California. She was staying with Dink's family while her parents were helping to build a Native American school in Arizona.

Bradley had a pad of paper and a pencil. "Okay, we need some ideas for how to dress Pal," he said. "I want to be mayor for a day!"

Pal was licking the edge of the pad.

Lucy was sitting next to Pal. "Do you want to be in the July Fourth parade?" she asked him.

Pal woofed a doggy *yes*.

"Are you going to win first prize?" Brian asked his dog.

Pal woofed twice as loud.

"Come on, guys, we need ideas," Bradley said.

Pal had long, droopy ears, sad brown eyes, and short legs.

"How about making Pal a moose?" Nate asked. "I have some antlers from a Halloween costume."

"That would look silly," Lucy said.

"Besides, moose have long legs."

"We could dress Pal as a cowboy and have him ride Polly in the parade," Brian suggested. "Like Roy Rogers and Trigger."

Polly, the Pintos' pony, was in her stall at the other end of the barn.

Bradley laughed at his brother's suggestion. "They'd both hate it," he said. "But you gave me an idea!"

"I did?" asked Brian.

Bradley nodded. "Yep. Just think, if we entered both Pal and Polly, we'd have two chances to win," he said.

"That's what I just said," Brian stated. "Pal can be a cowboy riding on Polly. Perfect!"

"But it's a July Fourth parade," Bradley said. "They didn't have cowboys in 1776."

"What did they have?" Nate asked.

"They had dinosaurs!" Brian yelled.

"We can dress Pal as a stegosaurus and Polly as a pterodactyl!"

The other kids laughed, and Bradley threw some hay at his brother.

"They did not have dinosaurs in 1776," Bradley said.

"Besides, if we want to win, we need the costumes to have something to do with Independence Day," Lucy said.

"Lucy's right," Bradley said.

"So we dress Polly as King George?" Nate asked. He started laughing and rolled over in the hay.

"My idea," Bradley said, "is to dress Polly as Thomas Jefferson. And Pal goes as the Declaration of Independence."

Brian stared at his brother. "I don't get it," he said.

"Bri, Thomas Jefferson wrote the Declaration of Independence," Bradley said. "Pal and Polly will be perfect, and

it stays with the theme of the parade! We could win!"

Lucy looked at Pal. "I think that's a great idea!" she said. "But how do we make Pal look like a sheet of paper?"

"I know!" Nate said. "I'll ask my sister to find a copy of the Declaration of Independence on our computer and print it out. Then we tie it on Pal's back, like a cape."

Brian grinned. "What about Polly?" he asked. "Thomas Jefferson had only two legs, and he wore pants. How do we make Polly look like him?"

"Easy," Bradley said. "We forget her hind legs. We put a wig on her head, with one of those funny hats with three corners. . . ."

"Like Mr. Vooray was wearing yesterday," Lucy put in.

"Right," Bradley said. "We can make some buckles and tape them to Polly's front hooves. It'll be so cool! Everyone will know who she's supposed to be, and we'll win the prize. I'll be mayor for a day!"

"No, *we* will," Brian said. "We can each be half a mayor."

"Not so fast," Nate said. "There are four of us here, so we each get to be a fourth of a mayor. I want to be his fingers so I can count all his money."

"I'll be his feet so I can drive his car," Bradley said.

"I hear the mayor likes to eat ice cream," Brian said. "I'll be his stomach!"

"How about you, Lucy?" Bradley asked.

"I'll be the mayor's brain," she said. "Then I control all of you guys!"

3

Pet Dress-Up

The kids spent the next few days gathering what they would need to turn Polly and Pal into Thomas Jefferson and the Declaration of Independence. On the morning of July Fourth they met on Bradley and Brian's back porch. Pal lay under a small table with his eyes closed. It was a sunny, warm day.

Nate had brought cardboard and a large sheet of paper. Printed on it was a copy of the Declaration of Independence. "Ruth Rose printed it out," he told the

others. "She's going to enter her cat,
Tiger, in the pet parade. She wants to be
mayor for a day, too!"

"No way!" Brian yelled.

He handed Nate some string and a
small bottle of glue.

"Pal will hate this," Brian said. "I
tried to dress him as Superman for
Halloween once, and he chewed on his
costume."

Hearing his name, Pal opened one
eye, yawned, then closed it again.

Lucy showed them a fluffy white wig.
"Dink lent it to us," she said. "He said he
was George Washington in a school play
once. He told me he's entering Loretta, his
guinea pig. Dink wants to be mayor, too!"

"There are hundreds of people with
pets in Green Lawn," Brian said. "They'll
all try to win!"

"So we have to make sure Pal and
Polly are the best," Bradley said.

"Look what I found in our attic," Brian said. He flopped an old-timey hat on his head. "I think it was my grandfather Pinto's."

"Dude, it needs to have three corners," Nate said. "This one is round."

"It will have corners when I'm done with it!" Brian said. He showed them his mother's sewing scissors. "I'll make corners."

"What else do we need?" Bradley asked.

"A ribbon for Thomas Jefferson's ponytail," Lucy said. "I looked him up, and he always wore one." She pulled a black ribbon from her pocket. "My aunt gave it to me."

"And we need buckles for his shoes," Nate said.

"Easy!" Brian said. He ran into the

kitchen and came back with a roll of tinfoil. "I figure we can cut buckles from some of this cardboard, then cover them with tinfoil."

"How do we keep them on Polly's feet?" Nate asked.

Bradley showed them a roll of tape. "Duct tape. It sticks forever."

"Duck tape?" Nate said. "Why do ducks need tape?"

"I think they're two different words," Bradley said.

"Listen," Lucy said. "I hear drums!"

"It must be the high school band practicing. The parade starts in an hour," Bradley said. "Let's get this stuff ready!"

Bradley started cutting two squares from Nate's cardboard. They *sort of* looked like buckles.

Lucy made a ponytail on the back of the white wig and tied the ribbon on to it.

Brian started snipping off pieces of

the hat, trying to make it look like Mr. Vooray's.

Nate poked two holes at the top of his copy of the Declaration, and two more near the bottom.

"What're the holes for?" Brian asked.

"For the string, so we can tie the paper to Pal's collar and around his tail."

Brian shook his head. "I don't know if Pal will like that, Nate," he said.

"Maybe we shouldn't try to put it on him until the parade starts," Lucy suggested.

"Good idea," Bradley said. "Okay, let's go show Polly her Thomas Jefferson wig!"

4
Polly Says No

The kids walked to the barn. Pal led the way with his tail wagging. Polly the pony was nibbling on straw in her stall. When the kids came near, she looked at them with big brown eyes. She let out a soft nicker and her ears went straight up.

Bradley stepped into the stall and slipped a halter over Polly's head. She playfully bumped her head against his and brushed his cheek with her soft lips.

"We'll need to make holes in the wig for her ears," Bradley said.

"Got it," Lucy said. Brian handed her the scissors, and he turned the wig inside out. The inside was stretchy cloth. With Brian holding the wig, Lucy cut two holes big enough for two pony ears.

"Let's try it on her," Brian said.

Bradley held the harness while Brian and Lucy slipped the wig onto Polly's head. Brian reached underneath and popped her ears up through the two holes.

"How does she look?" Lucy asked.

"Like a pony with a wig on," Nate said.

Suddenly Polly snorted and threw her head back. She stamped her feet on the stall floor.

"I knew she wouldn't like it," Bradley said. He pulled the wig off. "Settle down, girl."

Polly quieted right down. But she kept her eyes on the wig in Bradley's hand.

"Okay, I guess we won't put Polly's costume on until the last minute, either," Bradley said.

"I think we should tie the hat to the wig," Lucy said. "Then we can just plop the whole thing on her head when we get to the parade. We can tie it on with more of the ribbon."

"Good idea," Brian said. "And we can tape the buckles on her hooves at the same time."

"Okay, we have to go," Bradley said. He started to lead Polly out of her stall.

"Not so fast!" a voice said from the barn door. It was Josh, the twins' older brother. He was still in pajamas. "Mom and Dad said I have to go to the parade with you guys."

"We don't need a babysitter!" Brian squawked.

"No one's talking about a babysitter," Josh said. "I'll just be there in case anything goes wrong."

"Nothing is going to go wrong," Bradley said. "It's a parade!"

"Don't argue," Josh said. "I'm only doing what Mom and Dad told me. I'm meeting Dink and Ruth Rose there, anyway."

Nate giggled. "In your jammies?" he asked.

"Duh," Josh said. "I need to grab some breakfast and change."

"We have to go now!" Bradley said. "We can't be late for the pet parade!"

Josh thought for a minute. "Okay, go ahead," he said. "I'll catch up with you on the trail!" He turned and sped across the backyard.

"What's the trail?" Lucy asked.

"Come on, we'll show you," Brian said.

They cut through the meadow that surrounded the twins' house. Grasshoppers and butterflies flew into the air as their feet disturbed the tall grasses. Bradley held Polly's harness lead, and Brian held Pal's leash. Nate and Lucy carried the wig, hat, buckles, and Declaration of Independence.

They crossed Woody Street and walked between two thick posts on the other side.

"This is the trail," Brian said. They were standing in a clearing. Years of hikers walking there had worn the ground smooth. A path led south. They could see the high school buildings.

"Our dad looked it up," Bradley said. "The Mohegans used to walk here!"

"That's a Native American tribe, right?" Lucy asked.

"Yup," Nate said. "Mr. Vooray told us they had farms near here. They fished in the river!"

The kids followed the smooth trail through the high school grounds and past

Crystal Pond. A sign by the pond said
DUCK CROSSING. The trail ended next to the
veterinarian's office on East Green Street.

They saw Dr. Henry hurry down his
front steps. He was wearing a straw hat
and a red, white, and blue bow tie.

"Hi, Dr. Henry," Brian said. "Are you
going to the parade?"

"I have to miss it this year," Dr.

Henry said. "The petting zoo is having
a Fourth of July party for all its animals,
and they asked me to help out." He
looked at Polly and Pal. "I'll bet you're
entering the mayor's contest."

"Yes, and we're gonna win!" Brian
crowed. "We want to be mayor for a day!"

"Well, good luck to you," the vet said.

They all walked to the town baseball

field, where the parade would begin. Dr. Henry waved good-bye and crossed Main Street toward the petting zoo.

Most of the people in Green Lawn were already there. The baseball field was packed! Pal barked at a bunch of Boy Scouts and Girl Scouts standing on a float. Some firefighters were polishing one of their fire engines. The high school band members were making a lot of noise with their instruments.

Suddenly the mayor began yelling through a bullhorn, telling everyone to line up with their pets. His assistant, Mr. Grimaldi, stood next to him, holding a sign that said PET CONTEST HERE.

"Let's go," Bradley said. They led Polly and Pal toward the mayor.

About twenty people with their pets were already there. The kids saw dogs, cats, birds, and even a turtle. Each pet had on a hat or little costume of some sort.

"Ours are going to be better," Nate whispered.

"Look, there's your sister and Dink," Brian said. The kids waved at Ruth Rose and Dink, and they waved back.

Ruth Rose carried her cat, Tiger, in her arms. Tiger was wearing a strange hat, and she kept chewing on the string.

Dink held his guinea pig, Loretta. She had on a tiny mask, making her look like a raccoon.

Josh ran up, all out of breath.

Just then, the mayor announced that the pet contest would begin in three minutes. "ALL PETS AND THEIR OWNERS MUST LINE UP NOW!" he yelled through his bullhorn.

Lucy and Brian tied the three-cornered hat to the wig. Bradley set the wig on Polly's head and tied it on. Then he and Lucy taped the tinfoil buckles on to Polly's front hooves.

Nate and Bradley laid the Declaration of Independence on Pal's back like a cape. They tied it to his collar and tail.

"They look awesome!" Bradley said.

"I sure hope the mayor thinks so," Nate said.

"ONE MORE MINUTE!" the mayor cried.

Everyone turned to look at him.

And that was when Polly and Pal took off running.

5
No Parade for Polly and Pal

"Stop, Polly!" Bradley yelled. He watched as his two pets hurried away. They crossed Main Street and disappeared behind the Shangri-la Hotel.

"Bad pets!" Brian yelled after the fleeing animals. "No treats tonight!"

"Come on!" Bradley yelled. "We have to catch them!" He sprinted through the crowd. The other kids followed him.

On the other side of Main Street, they ran behind the hotel. They saw the senior center, the library, and the town hall. But they didn't see Polly or Pal. "Check in all the bushes!" Bradley yelled.

The kids scattered and began poking through the shrubbery. They scared out a few birds and one rabbit, but no pony or dog.

Bradley studied the ground. He knelt down for a closer look. "These are hoofprints!" he shouted. "Polly ran this way!"

The kids stood in the hot sun and looked around.

"Maybe she and Pal went into the hotel and got a room," Nate said. "Maybe they called room service and got cookies and lemonade!"

"Don't say *lemonade*," Brian complained. "I'm thirsty, and it's about a million degrees out here!"

"Polly and Pal must be thirsty, too!" Bradley said. "Maybe they went to the river!"

The kids raced past the library and crossed the bike path to reach the edge of the river. They looked up and down the river. A few ducks sped away, but Polly and Pal weren't there.

"Where could they get to so fast?" Lucy asked. "It's like they disappeared!"

"This is bumming me out," Brian said. "I was already planning my mayor's speech!"

"Guys, we won't win unless we find Polly and Pal!" Nate reminded them.

Bradley looked to the right, shielding his eyes against the sun. Then he peered to the left. "The sun is hot," he said. "Maybe they headed for the woods, where it's shady."

The kids hurried north along the bike path. They kept their eyes moving, checking both sides of the path and the river on their left. They stopped in the woods. They were all out of breath.

They peered through the trees on both sides of the bike path. "Check for hoofprints," Bradley said. But they saw no prints and no runaway pony.

"I'm still thirsty," Brian said. "When I'm one-fourth mayor, I'll have soda pop every day!"

"One-fifth, you mean," Bradley said. "Josh says he has to be one-fifth of the mayor, because he's part owner of Polly and Pal."

"No fair!" Brian yelped. "He didn't

even us help make the costumes!"

"Guys, let's not argue!" Lucy said. "We have to keep looking!"

Bradley held up a finger. "Wait," he said. He stood still, closed his eyes, and sniffed the air.

The others looked at him.

"I smell horse manure," Bradley said. His eyes snapped open. "The horseback-riding place is up there!" He pointed along the bike path. "Maybe Polly and Pal went to visit the other horses!"

"Let's go check it out," Brian said.

The kids started jogging up the path.

It was hot, and they were sweating.

"I need a chocolate milk shake, and I need it right now!" Nate said.

"We're almost there," Bradley said, pointing to a sign on the side of the trail. It said: RIDING TRAIL. WATCH FOR FAST HORSES!

"Watch for manure, too," Brian said.

Nate heard the noise first. "I hear drums," he said.

"Or thunder," Brian said. "Great, it's gonna rain!"

"No, I think it's horse hoofbeats," Lucy told him.

"You're right," Bradley said. "Look!"

Three horses with riders came galloping along the trail. The riders said, "Whoa!" and pulled up their mounts.

Two of the riders were men wearing cowboy hats. The third was a woman with red hair tied in pigtails.

"Hey, kids," the woman said with a smile. "Going riding?"

"No, we're looking for our pony," Bradley said. "And our dog. They ran away. Have you seen them?"

"What do they look like?" one of the men asked.

"They're both brown with white markings," Brian said.

"There are some brown ponies back at the stables," the other man said.

"Our pony's name is Polly," Nate said. He grinned. "She was wearing a white wig and a hat."

6

Vanished into Thin Air

"What?" the second man said. "Your pony wears a wig?"

"Um, they were dressed for a Fourth of July contest," Bradley said. "Polly was supposed to be Thomas Jefferson. Pal— he's our dog—had a big Declaration of Independence on his back."

"This sounds more like an April Fools' Day trick," the woman said. But she was smiling. "Try the stables next to the barn. Ask for Bucky, the stable manager."

"I hope you find them," the first man

said. "Giddyup!" he told his horse.

The three horses trotted away.

The kids hurried up the horse trail. Soon they saw a red barn with a stable off to one side. Horse heads and necks stretched out over some of the stall doors. The stable yard was busy with workers and people who had come to ride the horses.

"I wonder which one is Bucky," Brian said.

Bradley stopped a guy who was carrying a bale of hay toward the stables. "Excuse me, are you Bucky?" Bradley asked.

The man laughed. "Not hardly," he said. He pointed with his chin. "That's her in the pink shirt."

"Bucky is a girl?" Brian said.

The man let out a loud laugh. "Don't let *her* hear you calling her a girl!" he said.

The kids walked over to the woman in the pink shirt. She was old enough to be a grandmother. Her skin was tanned and her arms looked strong. She was wearing a baseball cap and sunglasses.

"Can I help you kids?" the woman asked.

"We're looking for a pony," Bradley said.

"I got plenty of ponies," Bucky said. She gave the kids a once-over. "You're not old enough to ride alone. Where are your parents?"

"We didn't come to ride," Lucy said. "Our pony and dog ran away and we wonder if they came here."

"Polly's wearing a hat and wig," Nate said.

"Who's Polly?" Bucky asked.

"Our pony," Brian said. "We dressed her for a contest. If we win, we get to be mayor for the day!"

Bucky stared at Brian. "You kidding me?" she asked.

"It was for the July Fourth parade," Bradley explained. "But Polly and our dog took off before it even started. Have you seen them?"

Bucky shook her head. "Nope. But

stroll over to the stables," she said. "I s'pose your pony might've snuck in there when I wasn't looking."

Bucky walked away, shaking her head. The kids raced for the stables. The stalls on the right held tall horses. But there were five ponies on the left.

One was white. One was black. Three were brown. None of them looked anything like Polly.

"She's not here," Bradley muttered.

Nate gazed at the other ponies. "They look like they know something," he said.

"Yeah, they know someone else is gonna be mayor for a day," Brian said. "The contest must be over by now."

The kids left the stable yard and took the bike path back to Bridge Lane. They kept their eyes open for any sign of Polly and Pal.

"How can a pony and dog just disappear?" Bradley asked.

"They didn't disappear," Lucy said. "They have to be somewhere we haven't looked."

"Right," Nate said, "like up in a tree or down a rabbit hole."

"No," Brian said. "We haven't looked in the most logical place yet."

"And where is that, brother?" Bradley asked.

"Home," Brian said. "Maybe Polly just went home. She could have run back to our house while we were searching everywhere else."

"Brilliant!" Nate said.

"Thank you, thank you," Brian said, taking a little bow.

Bradley poked his brother. "I hope you're right!" he said.

"I'm always right!" Brian crowed.

"You're never right!" Nate said.

The kids took off running.

By the time they reached Bradley and Brian's house on Farm Lane, they were all panting and dying of thirst. Brian turned on the outside faucet and they took noisy drinks.

Then the kids ran to the barn. It was quiet and cool and empty.

"I don't see her," Lucy said.

"What about the pasture?" Brian asked.

The kids dashed through the door and around to the back of the barn.

They bumped into Josh, Dink, and Ruth Rose.

The three older kids did not look happy.

7
The Police Join the Search

"Where have you been?" Ruth Rose asked, glaring at Nate. "We've looked for you kids all over town!"

"You had us worried," Dink said, giving his cousin a look.

"You were supposed to stay with us," Josh said.

"But we were looking for Polly and Pal," Bradley said. "We searched all over town, but we can't find them!"

"We've been looking, too," Josh said.

"Um, do you know who won the

mayor's contest?" Brian asked his older brother.

Josh grinned. "Your teacher, Mr. Vooray," he said. "He dressed his parrot like King George."

"Rats!" Nate said.

Bradley headed for the house. "We have to call Officer Fallon," he said over his shoulder. "I don't care about the contest anymore. My pony and dog are missing!"

All seven kids crowded into the kitchen. Josh poured glasses of water for everyone while Bradley looked up the number and dialed.

When he heard Officer Fallon's voice, Bradley explained what had happened to Polly and Pal. He told him how they had dressed them for the contest.

"No, I'm not joking," Bradley said.

Bradley listened, then hung up. "No

one has called in about Polly or Pal," he said. "But Officer Fallon said we should put up a bunch of signs around town. He said if we bring him pictures of Polly and Pal, he'll make a bunch of copies for us."

"That's a good idea," Ruth Rose said. "That way, everyone in town will know they're missing and start looking."

"Okay, you kids go see Officer Fallon," Josh said. "Dink and Ruth Rose and I will go knocking on doors."

Ten minutes later, Bradley and Brian, Nate, and Lucy climbed the steps to the police station. Bradley had found a nice picture of Polly and Pal together. It showed them near the barn.

The kids found Officer Fallon sitting at his desk, sipping from a glass of lemonade. A plate of cookies sat on a pile of papers.

"Come on in, gang!" the police chief said. "Grab a cookie and park yourselves

over there." He pointed to a long sofa. "So you've misplaced your pets, eh?"

The kids each took a cookie and sat on the couch.

"They ran away," Bradley said. "We were getting them dressed for the mayor's contest, and they just took off."

Officer Fallon grinned and tugged on his mustache. "Maybe they didn't like their outfits."

Bradley stood and showed him the picture of Polly and Pal near the barn. "Is this good enough to make copies?" he asked.

Officer Fallon reached across his desk and took the picture. "It's perfect," he said. "Give me a few minutes." He got up and left the room, then stuck his head back in the door. "And don't steal my cookies, or I'll have to put you in jail!"

Nate giggled. After Officer Fallon left, he whispered, "I wonder if he counted them."

"Don't even think about taking another one," Bradley said.

"Where should we bring the pictures?" Lucy asked.

"All up and down Main Street," Brian said.

Nate was wandering around the police chief's office.

"Don't touch anything," Bradley whispered.

"I'm not," Nate said. He stopped in front of a row of pictures of wanted criminals from around the state and the country. "Look at these guys. I'm glad none of them live in Green Lawn!"

Brian ran over to look. "Murderers and robbers and kidnappers," he said, shivering.

"Guys, you don't suppose someone kidnapped Polly and Pal, do you?" Lucy asked.

Three pairs of big eyes stared at her.

8

They're Really Gone!

"But I saw them running away," Bradley said. "Besides, who'd kidnap a pony and a big, fat basset hound?"

"This guy would!" Nate said. He tapped one of the wanted pictures. "He's big enough to pick up both of them and carry them away!"

"But you're forgetting one thing," Brian said. "That guy's not in Green Lawn."

"How do you know he's not?" Nate whispered. "He could be hiding in your basement! He could be waiting for you to go to sleep so he can creep up—"

Just then Officer Fallon walked back into the room.

All four kids jumped.

"What's the matter?" Officer Fallon asked. "You look like you've seen a monster."

"We have," Bradley said, grinning at Nate.

"Here's a bunch of pictures," Officer Fallon said, handing the pile to Bradley. "I added some stuff on the bottom."

Bradley read from the top photo: "Polly the pony and Pal the pooch are LOST! If you see them, call the police chief for a reward. 860-555-1007."

"We don't have any money for a reward," Brian said.

"I do," Officer Fallon said. He winked. "Now go out and paper the town with those pictures."

The kids thanked Officer Fallon and

Polly the pony and
Pal the pooch
are
LOST!

If you see them, call the
police chief for a reward.
860-555-1007

hurried back outside. Bradley handed each of them some pictures and kept the rest for himself. "Let's walk up Main Street and hand one to everybody we see," he said. "All the stores, too. We'll meet in front of the library when we run out of pictures, okay?"

"Nate, you and I will take this side of Main Street," Brian said. "Brad, you and Lucy hit the other side."

With a plan and a pile of pictures, the kids took off. Bradley and Lucy walked to the gas station first. They found the owner, Mr. Holly, fixing a flat tire. His face was smudged with grease marks.

"Hey, kids, what's up?" the jolly man said.

"Our pony and dog ran away and we're looking for them," Bradley said. He handed Mr. Holly a picture of Polly and Pal.

"Golly, Polly is lost?" Mr. Holly said.

"If they stop in, I'll give the police a call!"

The kids thanked him and ran next door to the Book Nook. Mr. Paskey took a picture as well, and hung it in his front window. He promised to keep an eye peeled for the missing pets.

Across the street, Bradley could see Nate and Brian coming out of the Green Lawn Savings Bank. He waved and they waved back.

"Howard's Barbershop is next," Lucy said.

"Good," Bradley said. "Howard can hand pictures out to his customers."

Pretty soon Bradley and Lucy were almost out of pictures. Bradley had given his last one to Ron Pinkowski. Mr. P, as the kids called him, owned Ron's Bait Shop. He promised to watch out for Polly and Pal.

"Well, I guess we go to the library and wait for the other guys," Bradley said. "I can't believe no one saw Polly!"

"I saved one picture for the library," Lucy said. "The librarian can show it to everyone who checks out a book!"

"Great idea," Bradley said.

When they reached the library, Lucy went inside with the picture.

Bradley sat on the steps. While he waited, he thought about Polly and Pal. Where would they go? Were they hiding on purpose? Had they been kidnapped, as Lucy had suggested? Did they decide to go off on an adventure, like that mouse Stuart Little?

Lucy came out of the library and sat next to Bradley. "She's going to show the picture to all her patrons," she said.

Bradley nodded. He couldn't look at Lucy because he had tears in his eyes. "Maybe they ran away for good," he whispered.

9
Never Give Up

"No, they didn't!" Lucy said. "They have to be somewhere in Green Lawn. We can't give up, Bradley."

Just then Brian and Nate came loping past the town hall. They were out of breath and out of pictures.

"Well, we did all we could," Brian said. "Now I guess we just have to hope someone calls Officer Fallon."

The four kids flopped on the grass under a tree.

"You're right, Lucy," Bradley said.

"We can't give up on this."

"But we've looked everywhere," Brian said. "My brain is tired."

"What brain?" Bradley teased, tickling his brother under the arm.

Brian threw a handful of grass at Bradley.

"Ponies and dogs aren't stupid," Bradley said, wiping pieces of grass off his T-shirt.

"Nobody said they were," Brian said. "So what?"

"So they wouldn't just wander around," Bradley went on. "They'd have a plan."

"Yeah, only they didn't bother to tell us what it was," Nate said.

"What do they both like to do?" Bradley asked. "What do Polly and Pal like better than anything?"

"Food!" the other three kids yelled, and they all laughed.

"Right," Bradley said. "So who do we

know who gives food to animals?"

"We do," Brian said.

"No, I mean other people," Bradley said.

"Dr. Henry, the vet, does," Nate said.

"And Mrs. Wong, at the pet shop," Brian said. "She even feeds squirrels and pigeons!"

"Did anyone bring them a picture of Polly and Pal?" Nate asked.

"Bradley and I tried at Dr. Henry's, but he wasn't there," Lucy said. "The place was closed."

"We stopped at the Furry Feet Pet Shop, but Mrs. Wong's shop was closed, too," Brian said.

"Well, I think we should try them again," Bradley said. "They both keep a lot of pet food around. Polly and Pal would smell it."

"We've tried everything else," Brian said. "Let's go."

The kids hiked back across Main Street and up East Green Street. They tried the front door of Dr. Henry's office, but it was locked. They walked all around the building. Bradley checked the ground for hoofprints.

"Okay, let's go to Furry Feet," he said.

The Furry Feet Pet Shop was on the corner of Main and Oak Streets. The kids stood in front of the shop, peering through the glass. They saw kittens, fish, and hamsters. No pony. No basset hound.

"The note's still on the door," Nate said. He read it: "At the petting zoo."

Bradley stared at the note. "Remember when we saw Dr. Henry this morning, on the way to the parade?" he asked the others. "He said he was going to help out at the petting zoo. And this note says Mrs. Wong is there, too."

"The vet said there was a party there for the animals today," Lucy said.

"Right, now I remember," Bradley said. He looked at the other kids.

"If there's a party for animals, there'll be food for animals. We should check it out."

The kids cut across Oak Street and

passed People's Pond. They hurried past the police station, library, and senior center.

"Wow, the place is crowded!" Nate said. Hundreds of people were at the Children's Petting Zoo and Aquarium. Almost everyone had a pet with them.

Many of the kids had party hats on.

There was a lot of noise from the animals and the people. Everyone seemed to be having a good time.

"Look, there's Mr. Neater," Brian said. He waved at a tall man with white hair. Mr. Neater used to be the janitor at their school. Now he worked as a volunteer at the petting zoo.

Mr. Neater was holding his rabbit, Douglas.

"Hey, kids, welcome to the party!" Mr. Neater said. "It's our own Fourth of July celebration."

The kids looked around. They saw

Mrs. Wong talking to some children while she fed baby ducks.

Dr. Henry was there, too. He was showing some kids how to brush a lamb's wool.

"Your pony and dog are here somewhere," Mr. Neater said.

"They *are*?" Bradley asked.

"Didn't you know?" Mr. Neater asked.

"We've been looking for them for hours!" Bradley said. "They ran away from the parade!"

"Goodness, they've been here all this time," Mr. Neater said. "My friends Ted and Sally have been watching them. We were wondering why you kids weren't here, too."

Bradley laughed. "We've been running all over town!" he said.

"Follow me," Mr. Neater said. Carrying Douglas in his arms, Mr.

Neater led the kids over to a small barn. Lots of people were there, feeding a flock of goats and some chickens.

Polly was being brushed by an elderly couple. A little girl was feeding her carrots and apples. Polly looked very happy.

Pal lay on the ground next to Polly's feet. He was watching some baby chicks pecking in the grass.

"Polly looks like a pony again," Bradley said.

Mr. Neater laughed. "Oh yes, we got rid of that funny wig and hat," he said. He looked at the kids. "Let me guess. You dressed them for the mayor's contest, right?"

Bradley nodded. "Yeah, and they hated it," he said. "I think that's why they ran away."

"They look happy now," Lucy said.

"I still want to be mayor for a day,"

Brian grumped. "It was gonna be so cool!"

Bradley put his arm around his twin brother's shoulders. "When you grow up, you can run for mayor," he said.

"No one would vote for me," Brian said.

"I would!" Nate said.

"Me too!" Lucy added.

"And I definitely would vote for you, bro," Bradley said.

Polly whinnied and Pal barked.

"See, even Polly and Pal would vote for you," Bradley said.

He walked over and hugged his pets. "And no more costume contests for you two, I promise," he whispered.